A Donut in Time
A Hanukkah Story

A SARALEE SIEGEL BOOK

A Donut in Time

A Hanukkah Story

By Elana Rubinstein
Illustrated by Jennifer Naalchigar

In loving memory of Grandma Sue.
You are in every page of this book.
— E. R.

For Mum and Dad.
— J. N.

Apples & Honey Press
An imprint of Behrman House
Millburn, New Jersey 07041
www.applesandhoneypress.com

Text copyright © 2022 by Elana Rubinstein
Illustrations copyright © 2022 by Behrman House

ISBN 978-1-68115-588-3

Library of Congress Control Number: 2022930388
Design by NeuStudio
Edited by Dena Neusner
Printed in China

1 3 5 7 9 8 6 4 2

Contents

Our family restaurant
We live on the top floor
SIEGEL HOUSE
Uncle Sam
Me
Aunt Lotte
Zadie, my grandfather
Aunt Bean
My little cousin, Josh
Bubbie, my grandmother
My family

Chapter One
Yesterday's Lunch

I once looked up the word "nose" in the dictionary. Here's what it said: *a nose is the part of the face used for breathing and smelling.*

Ha!

I bet those dictionary people have never heard of a nose like *mine* before. See, my nose can do FAR more than just breathing and smelling. My nose can do extraordinary things . . . it's a super-nose.

Just last week, my nose took me on an incredible adventure.

It all started on the first night of Hanukkah. Zadie and I were cooking in the restaurant kitchen. The counters were covered in a mountain of latkes. And the air smelled of freshly fried donuts.

"Are you serious, Saralee?" asked Zadie, as he flipped another latke on the stove. "There's no way your nose can do *that*."

"Oh, I'm serious," I said.

Zadie is my grandfather. He's the head chef of Siegel House, our family restaurant. He has hair the color of salt and pepper. And he always smells the same—like peppermint with just the slightest bit of corned beef on rye.

"Okay, prove it then," said Zadie. "What did I eat for lunch yesterday? I sat right over there, at the kitchen island."

I grinned and walked over to the island. Then I squeezed my eyes shut and took a deep sniff.

Immediately my nose was brimming with the smells of the kitchen. I could smell every ingredient in the latkes on the counter: three russet potatoes, one-fourth cup of oil, an onion, one egg, a teaspoon of salt, and Zadie's secret ingredient—a cup of crushed potato chips. Then there were the *sufganiyot*, the Hanukkah donuts. Zadie had used a bunch of different fillings: chocolate marshmallow, salted caramel, creamy pistachio, and vanilla cream.

But those weren't the smells I was looking for.

Concentrating, I sniffed even harder. I wanted to smell something far, far away . . . something from *yesterday.*

Inside my nose, I could feel my smell-receptacles pushing harder, sniffing deeper. I sifted through the smells of the kitchen, going through them one at a time.

Come on, nose, I thought to myself. *Let's do this!*

Suddenly, a very faint smell brushed my nostrils. My super-nose began to buzz and tingle.

"Aha!" I cried, opening my eyes. "You had an everything bagel with cream cheese, lox, a slice of cheddar cheese, red onion, and a tomato. Then you ate a dill pickle and a handful of barbecue chips. Oh, and chocolate pudding for dessert."

Zadie's mouth dropped open.

"Did I get it right?" I asked.

Zadie just stared. "Wait . . . are you . . . Saralee, that was *amazing*. How could you possibly smell that?"

I shrugged my shoulders.

"Don't know," I said. "My super-nose is getting stronger, I guess."

Zadie scratched his head. "Golly, that's for sure."

Just then, the kitchen door flew open. My aunt Bean rushed toward the sink. Today she wore her kitty cat shoes and a hand sanitizer necklace (watermelon flavor, of course). Aunt Bean never goes *anywhere* without her hand sanitizer.

"There's a line of customers waiting out in the cold," she said breathlessly. "And cold air means germs, germs, GERMS!"

She grimaced, scrubbing her hands at lightning speed.

I peeked out the kitchen window. The line curved all the way down the sidewalk. The customers were bundled up in their winter coats, scarves, and hats.

Hanukkah is an amazing holiday at Siegel House Restaurant. For eight nights, we remember the bravery of the Maccabees, a small group of rebels in ancient Israel. They fought against the big Greek army so they could stay Jewish and free. To celebrate, my family lights the menorah and tries to make the world just a little bit brighter.

This year, Zadie put one of my original donut recipes on the Hanukkah menu—peanut butter and jelly donuts! I'd perfected the recipe down to the last dollop of strawberry jam.

Zadie turned off the stove and wrapped an arm around my shoulder.

"You know," he said, giving my nose a tweak, "your super-nose sure is getting powerful. Maybe it's time you learned where it came from?"

I blinked a couple of times.

Came from?

"My nose?" I asked. "What do you mean?"

But before Zadie could answer, Aunt Bean pointed to the clock.

"Five minutes 'til dinner time," she shouted frantically.

Zadie scrambled back to his workstation.

"All righty everyone, it's GO time!"

Around me, all my aunts and uncles rushed around the kitchen with last-minute preparations.

"But wait—" I started.

Only Zadie didn't hear me.

The first night of Hanukkah was in full swing. I guess my questions would have to wait.

Chapter Two

Grown in a Lab

For the next few minutes, we all scrambled around like crazy people. But at last, the tables were set, the decorations were finished, and the food was hot and ready to go. Finally, Zadie brought the menorah into the dining room.

"Two minutes left," he said, breathless.

This was the last step before opening the restaurant for the night. We all gathered around as Zadie struck the match. I stared at the soft, glowing lights as Zadie said the blessings.

Questions were still bouncing around in my mind.

What had Zadie meant? Where *did* my super-nose come from? I'd never actually thought about that before. Maybe I had had some sort of accident as a baby? Or maybe I was bit by a radioactive bug that gave me super-smelling abilities?

I moved closer to my grandfather as we watched the candles burn.

"Ummm, Zadie—" I said, trying to get his attention.

But it was too late! He was already rushing back toward the kitchen to start the next batch of latkes.

Suddenly, I felt a poke in my ear.

I whirled around.

"Just checking your temperature," said my little cousin Josh, holding a plastic thermometer in his hands.

I took a deep breath.

I love my little cousin, but sometimes he can

be really annoying. He thinks he's a doctor and carries around his toy doctor's bag wherever he goes. Tonight he wore his favorite white lab coat over his skeleton pajamas.

"Hey, can I ask you a medical question?" I asked, getting an idea.

Josh nodded.

"Where do you think my super-nose comes from?"

Josh stared at my nose. Then he pulled out his toy stethoscope and pressed it against one of my nostrils.

"Hmmmm," he said. "Well, you were probably born without a nose . . . so the doctor did an experiment on you. He grew the best-est, most powerful nose in a science lab and then glued it to your face."

I stared at him. Okay—maybe asking Josh was a mistake.

He doesn't *actually* know that much about medical stuff, seeing as he's only in kindergarten.

"Yeah . . . I seriously doubt doctors can glue noses to people's faces," I said.

Josh shrugged. "You never know."

A moment later, Aunt Bean put on her germ-protectant gloves and opened the door to the restaurant. Customers streamed inside.

The rest of the night was a blur of latkes, donuts, songs, and light. I made so many peanut butter and jelly donuts, I lost count. But all the while, I couldn't get my mind off my super-nose. Why did I have a nose like this? Where did my smelling powers come from?

Finally, after hours of work, the restaurant closed for the night.

I went looking for Zadie. I found him in the downstairs pantry, putting away the extra ingredients from tonight's dinner.

"So, what did you mean before, Zadie?" I asked him. "Where *does* my super-nose come from?"

Zadie carefully placed a jar of jam on the shelf. Then he looked up at me.

I bit my lip. "Please don't tell me a doctor grew it in a lab and then glued it to my face."

Zadie chuckled. "No, nothing like that."

"So, what is it? How did my nose get like this?"

Zadie's eyes got all sparkly. "Well . . . actually . . . super-noses run in our family. It's a family trait!"

Chapter Three
The Family Nose

"**W**ha—what?" I spluttered.

There were *other* people in our family with a super-nose? I'd never even thought of that.

Zadie grinned even wider. "My mom, your great-grandmother, had a super-nose too."

I couldn't believe my ears.

My great-grandmother had a super-nose? My great-grandmother had a *SUPER-NOSE!*

Suddenly, my heart felt all soft and warm— like one of those buttery rolls rising in the oven.

For my whole life, I'd never known another person with a nose like mine. I thought I was the only one.

"But . . . why didn't you tell me before?" I asked.

Zadie's smile wavered.

"It's complicated," he said. "I wanted you to develop your smell powers in your own way. Be your own person, you know? I didn't want you to compare yourself to her."

"Oh," I said.

Zadie cleared his throat. "But lately, I've noticed that your nose is getting so much stronger. I think it's time for you to learn your history, the story of your super-nose."

I took a deep sniff, trying to calm down. The pantry smelled of onions, and garlic, and jars of canned peaches.

I still couldn't believe this. A family trait!

Questions just poured out of me like water. "So what was her favorite food? Did she like to cook? Did she have a favorite flavor? What—"

"Woah, woah hold your horses," interrupted Zadie. "Let me start from the beginning. Her name was Golda. But everyone called her Gigi for short. She's the one who created Siegel House Restaurant."

"Really?"

"Oh yeah, almost everything here was her idea—the unlimited pickle bar, the glass cookie display, the sign on the door . . ."

I scratched my chin. It had *never* crossed my mind that someone had actually invented our family restaurant before. It's just always . . . been here.

"She was a force to behold," Zadie continued. "A lot of people doubted her. But Gigi had a dream, and she never quit. And her food could make you *feel* things—happiness, sadness, excitement. Gee, I wish the two of you could have met!"

All of a sudden, that warm buttery feeling faded away. I looked down, crossing my arms. It was cold down here.

"What's wrong?" asked Zadie.

Gigi was gone. I'd *never* meet her. She was the only other person in the world with a super-nose, and we would never get the chance to spend time together.

"I just . . . I just wish we could have met each other too," I said quietly.

"Now, hold on a minute," said Zadie. "I have just the thing to cheer you up."

He walked over to an old filing cabinet

in the corner of the pantry. When he opened the top drawer, a puff of dust floated through the air.

I sneezed (super-noses are extra sensitive to dust).

Zadie pulled out a folder from the filing cabinet. "Aha! Here it is—a collection of her best recipes."

He handed me the folder. It was old, and crinkled, and smelled like stale crackers ten years past their expiration date.

"I know she's not *actually* here with us," said Zadie. "But these recipes come straight from her heart. They might help you get to know her. Why don't you take a look?"

"Okay, I will," I said, clutching the folder close.

Zadie yawned. "I could tell you so many stories. But we've got seven more Hanukkah dinners ahead of us. I think it's time to hit the hay. We'll talk more about this soon."

We walked up the stairs together.

"Now, don't stay up reading too late," said Zadie with a wink. "You've got school tomorrow. And a busy afternoon too—those peanut butter and jelly donuts won't make themselves."

"Ok, Zadie," I laughed. "Good night."

"'Night, Saralee."

Chapter Four
Gigi's Hanukkah Donuts

Soon the house grew quiet. I lay in bed, flipping through Gigi's recipes. Across the room, Josh cuddled under his blankets, clutching his doctor's bag like a stuffed animal.

He mumbled something in his sleep about vitamins.

I squinted my eyes, trying to read in the dim light. There were so many recipes stuffed inside the folder.

Blintzes

Soups

Salads

Kugels

Knishes

And finally . . . desserts.

I shuffled through the dessert section. There were raspberry cream fudge balls, root beer flavored ice cream . . . oooh and a Hanukkah donut recipe.

I pulled that one from the pile.

Gigi's Hanukkah Donuts, it said at the top of the page in swirly writing. The ingredients were fascinating: ground hazelnuts, chocolate chips, mashed banana, and a peanut butter drizzle.

Hmmmm . . .

Maybe it wouldn't hurt to cook a little something . . . ?

I stuck a toe out of bed. Then a whole foot.

Should I . . . ?

Okay, so *technically* speaking, I'm not supposed to use the kitchen alone (seeing as I'm only ten). But Zadie *did* say that Gigi's recipes would help me get to know her. And plus, I'd never be able to fall asleep now. Gigi's Hanukkah Donuts just sounded so scrumptious.

Making up my mind, I pushed the covers away and tiptoed out of bed. I crept down the hallway toward the stairs. Quietly, I snuck into the kitchen. The room was lit only by a nightlight, and I itched to get started.

See, when I cook, it's like having a party inside my super-nose. As the different flavors come together, it reminds me of the symphonies Zadie listens to. There's low notes, high notes, unexpected twists and turns—it's pure magic.

I started with the dough, whisking together the water, oil, flour, eggs, salt, and sugar. Then I began the donut filling and glaze. I mashed the banana and ground the hazelnuts.

I took a deep sniff, savoring the smell of the recipe. *Ahhhh*, I thought. *Now* that's a donut.

As the scent swirled around my nose receptacles, I thought about Gigi. She had made this exact recipe once upon a time. Okay . . . so we'd never get to meet in person. But maybe now we were a little more connected? At one point in time, Gigi had smelled this exact same scent.

And *that* was the moment something strange began to happen. My super-nose started to buzz and tingle.

It was the same feeling I had gotten earlier when I had smelled Zadie's lunch from yesterday. Only this time, it was more intense. Suddenly, my nose buzzed like an electric toothbrush at super high speed!

What was going on?

I squeezed my eyes shut as the smell of Gigi's donut recipe took over my nose. The scent grew stronger and stronger until I couldn't smell anything else. It bounced around my nostrils, growing more powerful by the second.

Only . . . the smell was different now.

I could still smell the sweet banana and chocolate chips. But underneath all that was something else—a tinge of sadness, of *bitterness*.

What in the world?

All of a sudden, the buzzing in my nose just . . . disappeared.

I opened my eyes.

Goosebumps formed on my arms.

The scent of Gigi's donuts had formed into some sort of . . . of smell cloud.

I stared at it, my eyes growing wide. The smell cloud grew bigger and bigger until it hovered in front of me like a giant orb.

Holy guacamole! *What did I just do?*

Chapter Five
Smell Cloud

I grabbed the edge of the counter, trying to steady myself.

Was this real?

I tried closing my eyes and opening them again—but the smell cloud was still there.

Slowly, I moved forward, trying to get a closer look. Inside the smell cloud was a hazy image. I squinted my eyes, trying to see it, but I couldn't make it out.

The hair on the back of my neck prickled.

Should I touch it?

It was as if the smell cloud had heard my thoughts. The scent of Gigi's donuts began pulling me forward. I tried to stop, but the smell was just so powerful! My mouth went dry, and my hands grew clammy as I stepped straight *into* the smell cloud.

I gasped. I was . . . I was *inside* the smell of Gigi's Hanukkah Donuts. All around me, different ingredients flashed by. Bananas swirled around my head. Sugar, and eggs, and chocolate chips zoomed around and around. Globs of peanut butter whirled past me. And yet, I could still smell that bitter scent lurking beneath it all.

Then, everything began to spin.

It spun so fast, I held my breath and closed my eyes. And when I opened them again, I couldn't believe the sight.

The Siegel House kitchen was completely gone.

Frantically, I whirled around. The smell cloud was behind me now. Had I just traveled somewhere . . . inside of a smell? Like a doorway or portal? That seemed impossible!

I looked at my surroundings. I was in a very strange-looking kitchen. Everything looked so old— like something out of a history book. The walls were covered in minty-green wallpaper and there were checkered tiles on the wall.

"Who . . . who are you?" said a shaky voice.

I spun to my left. Standing at the kitchen counter was another girl.

She looked to be the same age as me, with red hair, the same color as mine, but shorter and curlier. She was wearing an apron over an embroidered nightgown.

She gawked at me, her eyes all wide.

For a moment, all I could do was stare back. It looked like she was cooking something. I took a tiny sniff. The whole kitchen smelled like Gigi's donuts.

"I . . . uhhh . . ." I started.

But the girl clutched her mixing spoon and held it in front of her like a shield. "How did you get inside my house?"

I didn't know what to say! This was just too weird. Okay, sure, I knew my super-nose was powerful. But I hadn't expected it to actually *transport* me somewhere! How could I explain that?

I stepped forward. "Well . . . I . . ."

The girl backed away from me.

"Help! Intruder!!" she yelped.

Suddenly, I could hear footsteps coming down the stairs. *Uh-oh!*

My heart started to race. I had to get out of here!

Fast as I could, I jumped back through the smell cloud. Again I was surrounded by flying bananas, swirling globs of peanut butter, and zooming chocolate chips. Everything began to spin, and I closed my eyes tightly, squeezing my arms around myself.

And when everything stopped moving, I peeked one eye open. I was back in the Siegel House kitchen.

I touched my nose with a shaky hand.

What had just happened?

Where had I gone?

Chapter Six
Sheet Cake

That night, I tossed and turned and tossed some more. I kept replaying what had happened over and over in my mind. I'd made Gigi's donuts . . . and then, *wham*, I'd traveled somewhere. Somewhere where things looked . . . different. I burrowed deeper under the covers.

Maybe all of this was just in my imagination?

The next morning, I was still in a daze as I walked to school. The air was so cold, my nose had turned completely pink by the time I sat down next to my best friend, Harold Horowitz.

"Hey Saralee, can I show you something?" he said as soon as he saw me. "I have an amazing Hanukkah cooking idea!"

I nodded. "Okay. Then I have something to tell you too."

Harold and his family own the other restaurant in town, Perfection on a Platter. We haven't always gotten along (seeing as our families compete over customers sometimes), but I'm glad we worked things out. Harold is the only other kid I know who loves cooking just as much as I do. Plus, he's a serious pastry artist. He makes these incredible cookies that he intricately paints with sugar icing. They are truly works of art.

Harold took out a piece of paper and handed it to me.

"Here's my blueprint," he said. "I want to make a sheet cake that tells the story of Hanukkah! What do you think?"

I looked down at the paper. Harold had

drawn a rectangle and illustrated the entire Hanukkah story inside.

"Is that the ancient Temple?" I asked. "Are you painting that with icing?"

He nodded. "Yeah, and I want to make the menorah flames out of yellow M&Ms."

"Who's that?" I asked, pointing to one of the figures on the cake.

"Oh, that's the Greek king telling all the Jews to stop being Jewish," said Harold. "I'm gonna make his clothes out of sour gummies . . . get it? Because he's the bad guy!"

I rolled my eyes. "Oh, I see. So let me guess, you're gonna make Judah Maccabee out of extra spicy Red Hots because he's so strong?"

Harold smiled. "You know, I hadn't thought of that, but it's a pretty good idea."

I wrinkled my nose. "I was just kidding, Harold. You can't have Red Hots and sour gummies on the same cake."

Harold pointed at a teeny tiny area of the blueprint. "This is my favorite part—I'm going to make a small oil jar out of caramel and put it somewhere in the candy Temple. Whoever finds the oil jar on their cake slice will get to light the menorah at our restaurant that night. Genius, right?"

I nodded. "Now I have something to tell you," I said in a low voice.

I looked around the classroom. Jacob Brodsky was sitting close to us, and I didn't want him to overhear.

"But you have to promise to keep it a secret. Okay?"

He raised his eyebrows. "Okay, promise."

"You know how my nose is pretty powerful and stuff?"

He nodded.

"Well, last night, my nose did something really crazy. I think it might have *transported* me somewhere."

Harold's eyes grew wide. "No way! That sounds impossible."

"I know," I said. "I traveled to this very old-looking kitchen. It was crazy. But maybe I just made it up in my mind, you know?"

Harold looked around to make sure no one else was listening. "I don't know, Saralee. Maybe it did happen? I've seen your nose do some pretty crazy things. Remember the Starlight Soup? That was incredible! And didn't you sniff out the secret ingredient to your zadie's apple cake?"

I shrugged. "True, but this seems different somehow."

"So, what are you going to do?" Harold asked. "Are you going to try it again? Then you'll know for sure if it was real."

33

I took a deep sniff. The classroom smelled of freshly sharpened pencils and the scent of wet glue.

"I don't know . . . I definitely scared the girl who was already there. She called me an intruder!"

Harold tilted his head to the side.

"Come on, Saralee," he said. "Don't you want to know what your super-nose can do? If I had a superpower like you do, I'd want to know everything about it."

"That's true," I said.

I thought about my super-nose. There was a lot I still didn't understand about it. I mean, until last night, I had no idea that super-noses ran in my family. What else didn't I know?

Riiiiiiiiing, went the morning bell.

"Tell me what happens if you try again," whispered Harold, as class started for the day. "Seriously, Saralee, your nose is the coolest."

Chapter Seven
Disaster Zone

All day I thought about what Harold said.

Maybe he was right?

Maybe I could make another batch of Gigi's donuts this afternoon and try the whole smell portal thing again?

But things weren't so simple. When I arrived home, the kitchen was packed with people. My whole family was getting ready for tonight's Hanukkah dinner. We had a big night ahead of us—the residents of the senior center, the Shalom Home, were coming as guests.

Zadie was frying some donuts on the stove. He carefully dropped balls of dough into a scalding hot pot of oil. They puffed up immediately and floated to the top, perfectly golden brown.

My uncle Sam was grating the potatoes for the latkes. His cheeks were all red as he shredded a potato at turbo-speed. His hands moved so fast, the potato slipped and went flying across the room.

"Oh snickerdoodle," he squawked.

The potato landed on the floor in front of Bubbie, my grandmother.

"Well, hello there, Pookie Wookie," Bubbie said to the potato. "Aren't you a cute puppy?"

She bent down to give the potato a pat.

Poor Bubbie is always a bit confused about things. She calls everyone Pookie Wookie because she's not so good at remembering names. Today she wore her nightgown like a fancy dress and one of her handmade macaroni necklaces.

Uncle Sam walked over and picked up the potato.

He patted Bubbie on the back. "Oh that's not a puppy. It's a potato! Want a latke? I'm making them fresh."

Bubbie nodded. "Of course, Pookie Wookie. Of course."

Meanwhile, my aunt Lotte stood at the sink pretending to wash dishes. Aunt Lotte is the

Siegel House waitress. She usually spends her time shouting orders into the kitchen at the top of her lungs. Everyone knows that she's a terrible dishwasher. She usually just runs the dishes under the water instead of actually scrubbing them.

Nearby, Aunt Bean was polishing the silverware. She kept looking over at Aunt Lotte, her eyes narrowing.

"Now Saralee Siegel," she said as soon as she noticed me. "Was that *you* who made a mess in the kitchen last night and didn't clean up?"

I blushed.

I guess with everything going on, I'd forgotten to put away all of the cooking stuff. "Sorry," I squeaked.

Aunt Bean shook her head but gave me a teensy tiny little smile. "Guess you can't take a true cook out of the kitchen," she said. "But no more cooking by yourself at night, understand?"

I nodded, swallowing hard.

Making another batch of Gigi's donuts just got more complicated. When else would I be able to use the kitchen alone?

That night went by without any luck. The guests from the Shalom Home seemed to order an endless stream of latkes and donuts. The restaurant was so busy, there wasn't a single quiet moment.

The same thing happened the next evening and the evening after that. By the time the weekend rolled around, my stomach was in knots. Would I *ever* get to make Gigi's donuts in the kitchen alone? It seemed like I'd never get the chance.

But finally, on Sunday morning, an opportunity arose.

"Now, let's skedaddle everyone. We've got a shopping list a mountain high," called Zadie. Everyone was putting on their winter coats and gloves to run errands. The restaurant was running low on a bunch of supplies.

"Where's Aunt Bean?" I asked, looking around.

"I'm not coming!" called a voice from the downstairs pantry. "These shelves are a mess. I don't know how you people can stand such a disaster zone. I'm spending the day organizing down here."

My eyes lit up.

I would never be allowed to stay home alone. But since Aunt Bean was staying . . . Aha!

"Ummm, Zadie," I said. "I don't think I

can come either. I have to . . . to do a project.

Zadie raised an eyebrow. "A project?"

"Ummm, remember that folder of Gigi's recipes you gave me?" I asked quietly. "There's a donut recipe I just *have* to make. You know, flavor research for my super-nose."

Zadie looked up at me. Then his eyes twinkled.

"Oh," he said. "I see. Make me some extra? Those recipes bring back so many memories— it's like time travel."

I froze in my spot. My heart seemed to skip a beat.

Time travel? Could that be what happened?

"Wait, Zadie—?" I spluttered. "What do you mean?"

But Zadie didn't answer me. He was already walking out the door, his feet crunching on the snow.

Chapter Eight
The Other Girl

A few minutes later, I stood in the kitchen completely alone. I could hear Aunt Bean thumping around in the downstairs pantry. But the rest of the house was quiet, peaceful.

My hands felt sweaty.

I mean, I know I have a super-power and everything. But time travel . . . that's crazy, even for me!

But before I could talk myself out of it, I gathered all of the ingredients together. I began the dough—flour, oil, eggs, sugar, water, and salt. Then I started on the donut filling. The scent of the bananas, chocolate, and hazelnuts filled the air.

This was it!

I wiggled my nostrils . . . waiting.

But nothing seemed to happen. So I gripped the bowl and whisked as fast as I could. I thought about Gigi making this exact same recipe a long time ago.

And suddenly, it happened again. My super-nose began to buzz and tingle!

The smell of Gigi's donuts grew overpowering. And there it was again . . . that hint of bitterness underneath the sweet.

In front of me, the smell cloud seemed to form out of nowhere.

My pulse began to race as the smell cloud grew bigger and bigger. And before I could change my mind, I did what I set out to do. I took a deep breath and stepped straight through.

"Stay away, you ghost!" cried a voice.

I blinked a few times, trying to steady myself. Again, I was in the old-fashioned kitchen. I whirled around to find the other girl standing at the kitchen counter, mixing something in a large bowl. Her hands were trembling, and her face was pale.

"Look, don't be scared," I said. "I'm not a ghost. I'm friendly, I promise!"

I gave her a smile, just to prove it.

"But how did you get here?" she whispered.

I swallowed, taking in the details of the room. I had been so overwhelmed last time, I hadn't noticed the menorah on the windowsill. It looked exactly the same as my menorah from home. And it had five blue candles waiting to be lit.

Well, I guess it was also Hanukkah wherever I was.

I turned back to the girl. "Do you . . . uhh . . . do you see the cloud thing?"

She nodded.

"Well, *that's* how I got here," I said. "I

traveled in it. I know that sounds weird, but I'm telling the truth."

The girl seemed to calm down a little.

I watched as she closed her eyes and took a deep sniff. It was like looking into a mirror. The way she wrinkled up her nostrils . . . it reminded me of what I do to try and activate my nose-receptacles.

"That's not a cloud," said the girl softly. "That's a smell . . . the smell of my Hanukkah donut recipe. I'm making it right now. How did you do that?"

My jaw dropped.

Wait, what?

Had I heard correctly?

I looked at the other girl's mixing bowl. She was making Gigi's Hanukkah Donut Recipe too. But that would mean . . .

"Did you say *your* recipe?" I gasped.

"Yes," said the girl. "I've been working on it for ages. I finally got it just right today."

I couldn't believe it. This was Gigi! My great-grandma, Gigi. The one with a super-nose.

The one who invented Siegel House Restaurant!
My mind scrambled to make sense of things.

Both Gigi and I had super-noses. So the
smell of Gigi's Hanukkah Donut Recipe must
have connected our noses—through TIME. It
was smell travel!

I looked back at the smell cloud. Through it,
I could see a small image of the Siegel House
kitchen. It was like I was looking at my home
from miles away.

"I ummm—I think I know who you are," I
started. "Is your name Gigi?"

The girl nodded. "How did you know that?"

For a moment, all I could do was stare. Gigi and I didn't look so different from each other. She was a bit smaller than me, and her clothes were much fancier. But we definitely looked related.

Gigi moved toward me.

"You promise you're friendly?" she asked. "Because you appeared out of nowhere, like a real ghost."

I nodded. "I promise. "You will never believe who I am. I'm—"

But before I could finish, the kitchen door flew open. A man walked into the room. He wore a blue suit with a matching hat.

I immediately ducked behind the counter. But the man didn't even glance in my direction.

"Gigi, the doctor is here," the man said.

From behind the counter, I could see Gigi's shoulders slump.

"Um, Father, do you notice anything strange in here?" she asked.

The man frowned. "Strange?"

Gigi nodded. "You don't see anything . . . out of the ordinary?"

The man tapped his foot impatiently. "What's this nonsense about? We can't keep the doctor waiting like this. You were late last week."

"I don't want to see the doctor," said Gigi.

But her father was having none of it. He ushered Gigi out of the kitchen and into the living room, where the doctor was waiting. I followed closely behind. I guess Gigi was the only person who could see me. No one else even glanced in my direction.

The doctor took out a notepad and pen. Gigi crossed her arms.

"Now, my dear," said the doctor. "Have you been doing your nose exercises? You must do them if you ever want your nose to function normally."

I gasped.

Function normally?

Was the doctor trying to take Gigi's super-nose powers away? Why would he want to do that?

Chapter Nine
The Doctor

I watched in horror as the doctor examined Gigi's nose.

Gigi's father paced nervously around the room.

"You've been doing your exercises, right, my darling?" he asked Gigi. "I'm sure we can fix this problem in no time."

"But I told you—" Gigi said quietly. "I like my nose as it is. And having a powerful nose is really going to come in handy."

"That's nonsense," said her father. "You have a malfunction, a disorder."

"But—it's true," she said. "Using my nose, I've finally perfected my Hanukkah donut recipe. I've been saving my money, and I have just enough to open a booth at the Hanukkah festival. I'm starting my own business. And hopefully, I'll have my own restaurant one day."

The doctor scribbled on his notepad. "Sir, you need to get your daughter under control. A business? A restaurant? This nose is putting ideas in her head. Who knows what else it will lead to!"

Gigi's face turned red. "But my nose—it can do so much! I can smell—"

"That's quite enough about your nose," snapped her father. "We've talked about this. Your nose *will* be cured."

Gigi looked down. She looked like she was close to tears. "Okay."

"Will you do your exercises, young lady?" asked the doctor. "From this day forward?"

He took out two clothespins from his pocket and handed them to her.

Gigi nodded. "Yes, sir."

Her father relaxed. "It's only because we care about you. Don't you want to live a regular life? Be like everybody else? Trust me, you don't want to have a business. It's not proper for a lady."

A tear slipped down Gigi's cheek. "Yes, Father."

I couldn't believe what I was hearing. Inside, I was boiling up like a tea kettle on the stove. Not proper for a lady? What did that even mean? I'm a girl, and Zadie always says there's *nothing* I can't do, that I'm unstoppable!

Plus, why were they picking on her super-nose? Super-noses are amazing. I wouldn't trade mine for anything on the planet. The things I get to experience—a rainbow of scents swirling around me at every moment . . . I couldn't imagine living any other way."

Gigi's father took out a pocket watch and frowned. "It's back to work for me. But since you have nothing to do today, this is an excellent opportunity for you to wear that clothespin on your nose for a while. Your mother will be so pleased when she returns home."

I watched as he walked the doctor to the front door. Gigi and I were left alone. She looked up at me.

"You know, I don't know who you are—but maybe it's time you went back to wherever you came from," she said sullenly. "I'm not having a very good day."

I stared at her.

THIS girl was the brave, unstoppable Gigi?

Zadie had told me that Gigi was the most courageous woman he'd ever met. That she always stood up for her dreams. But this Gigi didn't seem anything like that.

I had to say something. I had to do something!

"Look, Gigi," I said. "You can't get rid of your super-nose. You just can't!"

Gigi crossed her arms. "And how would you know anything about this? I don't even know who you are."

"Yeah, I actually do know a little something about super-noses," I said. "I have one myself."

Gigi's mouth fell open. "You do? But I thought I was—"

"The only one?" I filled in.

She nodded.

"Well—you're not going to believe this—but the reason we both have super-noses is because we're actually related."

"So you're my cousin?" Gigi asked.

I shook my head. "This is going to sound crazy. But I'm from the future. You're my . . . my—"

The words sounded so silly.

"You're my great-grandmother," I blurted.

Chapter Ten
Only Ten

Gigi put her hands on her hips. "Impossible. How can I be a great-grandmother? I'm only ten!"

"I promise you I'm telling the truth. What year is it now?" I asked.

"1936," said Gigi.

I sucked in a breath. Wow, I had time traveled pretty far back!

"Look, I'm from waaaaay in the future. Like seriously—our kitchen looks like a spaceship compared to yours. We have a microwave, a rice cooker, and a refrigerator."

Gigi's eyes grew wide. "Micro what?"

I laughed. "Microwave. It's this thing that can heat up your food in less than a minute."

"That's impossible. Who are you really?" she asked.

"Look," I said. "I can prove it to you. Having a super-nose is a family trait. You have one, and I have one—we're related."

I started walking back into the kitchen, and Gigi followed behind me. The smell cloud was still hovering in the air.

I pointed to the bowl sitting on the counter. "I can name every single ingredient in your donut dough just by taking a sniff."

"Okay, show me."

I smiled softly. Then I closed my eyes and took a little sniff. My nose immediately filled with Gigi's delicious donut recipe. "Your dough uses exactly one cup of water, one tablespoon of yeast, three cups of flour, one fourth cup of powdered sugar, one half teaspoon of nutmeg, three quarters teaspoon of salt, two large egg yolks, two tablespoons of oil, and one teaspoon of vanilla extract."

Gigi stared at me. "That's . . . that's correct."

She stepped closer to me. Then she blinked a few times. "You're really telling me the truth, aren't you?"

I nodded.

"Well—you did appear out of nowhere. And we do have the same color hair," Gigi said softly.

"And the same eyes," I said.

I stuck out my hand.

"I'm Saralee Siegel," I smiled. "I'm a master sniffer and chef at Siegel House Restaurant. It's nice to meet you, Great-Grandmother."

Gigi didn't reach out to shake my hand. Instead, she curtsied.

"How do you do?" she said. "I'm Gigi."

Chapter Eleven

Portal Problems

Gigi seemed nervous as she made a pot of tea. She set two china teacups, a small bowl with sugar cubes, a silver spoon, and four homemade chocolate biscuits on the counter.

"Wow," I said, looking at all the dishes. "So elegant. Do you use fancy teacups all the time?"

Gigi nodded. "When we have guests? Of course."

I took a nibble of the biscuit. It was flavored to perfection—a deep chocolate taste with orange zest and spice. But, just like the donut recipe, there was a tinge of bitterness underneath the sweet.

The flavor made my heart ache. It reminded me of all the times I felt sad and lonely.

"How do you do that?" I asked. "It's almost like there's *feelings* in your food."

Gigi sighed.

"It's not on purpose," she said. "But my feelings . . . they all seem to have flavors. Bitterness, spiciness, sweetness, and everything in between. On good days, my food makes everyone happy. But on bad days, my food just . . . makes everyone feel sad."

Wow, Zadie was right. Gigi's nose was incredibly powerful!

"Your super-nose is so strong," I gushed. "How could you ever want to give it up?"

Gigi darted her eyes away. "I don't *want* to give it up, but I'm starting to think that I don't have a choice."

"But why?" I asked. "Just because your dad and the doctor think you should?"

There was a moment of silence.

"It's not—it's not just them," she finally said. Then she crossed her arms. "I don't think you'll understand."

Gigi was right. I didn't understand!

"Well, what if I told you that you were going to create an amazing restaurant one day? I help out there myself. The townspeople love it. There's a pickle bar and a glass cookie display. We serve sandwiches bigger than your face."

Gigi looked down. "It's just a silly dream. It's probably never going to happen."

"But I just told you—"

I looked back at the smell cloud and did a double-take. It had . . . *changed*.

Sure, the image of the Siegel House Restaurant kitchen was still there. But it was more blurry and hard to make out. It was as if someone had smudged it with ink.

Uh-oh.

I took a step closer to the portal. Maybe it was time to go home? I didn't want to get stuck here . . . *for good*!

But terrible thoughts flashed through my mind. If Gigi never got the courage to start her own restaurant . . . would there even *be* a Siegel House Restaurant for me to go home to? Gigi was the one who had created Siegel House in the first place. Without her, would the whole restaurant just disappear?

I shivered.

There had to be something I could do about this!

"Gigi," I said in the strongest voice I could manage. "I'm going to show you how amazing your super-nose is. We are going to open your Hanukkah booth, and everyone's going to love it, I promise!"

Chapter Twelve
Nose Girl

It was a brilliant plan. With my help, Gigi would see that having a super-nose was awesome! She'd see that having her own business was possible. She'd get her big dream back—to own her own restaurant one day. And then I could go back to Siegel House Restaurant with the smell cloud. Easy peasy lemon squeezy.

"But my father said—" started Gigi.

I didn't let her finish. "He's wrong, okay? Look, with two super-noses working together, we can make the best donut menu this town has ever seen. Your dad will be so proud."

"But how do you know that?" she asked.

I beamed. "Last night, my restaurant served one of my original recipes—peanut butter and jelly donuts. Everyone said it was absolutely delicious. People love an exciting new donut flavor. Trust me."

"Well, okay, I guess," she said with a shy smile. "It *would* be nice to cook with someone else with a super-nose."

That warm, buttery feeling came back again. This was actually happening. I actually had the chance to cook with Gigi. We could discover different flavors and experiment with recipes just like I'd wanted. It was my dream come true!

Here's the thing about my super-nose: I always figured that my nose was one-of-a-kind. I never knew how much fun it would be to meet someone else with the same skills.

After finishing our
biscuits and tea, Gigi took me to the
grocery store. We needed some ideas for our
donut menu. The winter wind whipped our
faces as we raced down the street.

I took a deep sniff. I could smell the smoke
swirling out of the chimneys. I could smell the
evergreen trees swaying in the breeze. And then
there was the snow: fresh and sweet, falling to
the ground like powdered sugar.

Gigi's grocery store was *much* smaller than mine. There were no aisles. Just a wide-open room with shelves on the walls. We wandered through the sections, exchanging ideas.

"How about a donut with chocolate and pecans?" started Gigi.

My nose receptacles started to light up with flavor possibilities. "Yes! And what about adding a little vanilla and cinnamon for flavor?"

"Absolutely, with a hint of cherry?" asked Gigi.

My mouth started to water.

"Of course," I said. "And I was thinking about another donut—maybe some sort of citrus filling with orange and ginger?"

Gigi closed her eyes and breathed in deep. I could tell she was using her nose to imagine the flavor. "Oooh, with some sort of honey glaze!"

"Yes!" I cried. "Honey glaze is perfect."

We both sniffed inward at the same time. Then we both laughed.

"This is fun," she said. "It's like I've known you forever."

"Agreed," I said.

Ting a ling a ling, went the bell on the door.

We both looked up as two girls walked into the store. They were wearing knee-length dresses with lace trim. They had shorter hair like Gigi and looked to be about the same age as us.

Gigi frowned.

The girls looked Gigi up and down. Then they smirked at each other. I didn't think they could see me because they only looked at Gigi.

"Look, it's the nose girl," said the first girl.

Gigi blushed.

"What are you doing, nose girl? Sniffing all the food in the grocery store?" said the other girl, laughing.

I wrinkled my nose.

I mean, as a matter of fact, we *were* sniffing all the food in the grocery store. What was wrong with that? It's the best way to come up with recipe ideas.

"Hey," I said. "That's not very nice. Super-noses are the best."

But neither girl looked in my direction. They definitely couldn't see me.

"Come on, Saralee," Gigi whispered to me. "Let's pay and get out of here."

Chapter Thirteen
Better Together

Gigi and I left the store in a rush. Gigi carried our bag of groceries, her face still flushed. She didn't say much.

"Ummm, Gigi," I started. "Are you okay?"

"Yeah, I'm fine," she said, looking down at the sidewalk.

"Who were those girls?"

"Just people from school."

"Oh," I bit my lip. "And they all call you *nose girl*? That's so mean."

"I'm used to it," she said quietly.

I thought about my own family and friends. Not once had they made me feel different. If anything, they all were excited for me to use my nose in unique ways. I mean, just last night, Zadie put one of my dishes on the Hanukkah menu. He believed in me. He always had, and he always will. And Harold—he said that I had the coolest nose in the whole world.

I guess . . . I guess Gigi didn't have anyone like that.

I looked over at her.

Something just wasn't right. Zadie had said that Gigi always stood up for herself. That she was the fiercest and most courageous woman he'd ever met. Maybe Zadie was wrong? Maybe he didn't know Gigi as well as he'd thought?

"Well, who cares about them," I said. "They have no idea of all of the cool stuff that you can do."

Back in the kitchen, Gigi and I unloaded the shopping bags. We rolled up our sleeves and began to cook. The grocery store incident was soon forgotten.

I took a deep sniff, taking in all of our flavors:
Blueberry glaze
Chocolate pecan
Lemon and lime
Juicy fig
Coffee cream
Red velvet

And of course, Gigi's Hanukkah Donut recipe and my very own peanut butter and jelly donuts.

When it was time to sample the first batch, Gigi and I cut a donut in half. It was one of the recipes we'd made together.

"You ready?" asked Gigi.

I nodded.

We both took a bite, relishing the flavors. I could taste lemon, and honey, and vanilla extract. As the flavors swirled around my tongue, my heart began to feel all warm and fuzzy. The feeling was just so strong!

"Did your super-nose do that?" I gushed. "All these feelings—it's such a rush."

Gigi blushed.

"I guess it's because you're here," she said. "Cooking with you just makes me so happy. I never thought I would meet someone like me."

I grinned at her.

I felt like I had found a piece of myself that I didn't know was missing. If I were grilled cheese, Gigi would be my tomato soup. If I were a pancake, she'd be the maple syrup.

We just went better together.

"Gigi, my darling," said a voice. "What on earth are you doing?

Chapter Fourteen
Hanukkah Festival

I whirled around.

A woman strode into the kitchen. She wore a long dress with clickety-clack heels. On her head was a black hat with a pink flower.

I knew immediately that this must be Gigi's mom. She had the same eyes and hair color as we did.

Gigi fidgeted. "Ummm... I made Hanukkah donuts, Mother. I made a whole menu of them. I'm... I'm going to open a booth at the

Hanukkah festival this afternoon. I'll sell my donuts there every day until Hanukkah is over. I'm starting a business."

The woman frowned.

She set down her pocketbook and walked over to Gigi.

"Oh my love," she said, tousling her daughter's hair. "You definitely have a gift for cooking. But you're not cut out for all that. Leave the businesses for the boys."

WHAT?

Leave the businesses for the boys? I couldn't believe what I was hearing. What did that even mean? I knew plenty of businesses owned by women. The shoe store on Main Street, the doctor's office, the furniture store—just to name a few.

The woman plucked a donut off the counter and took a bite. "Mmmmm, delicious. Gosh, it's like taking a bite of . . . of happiness."

The woman patted Gigi on the head, then headed toward the living room.

"Don't make too much of a mess, my

dear," she called over her shoulder.

When she was gone, Gigi bit her fingernail. Then she looked at me.

"Are you sure we should still do this?" she asked. "I mean the doctor and Father and Mother all said that—"

"I know what they said," I interrupted. "But I'm telling you, they're wrong! We've got to *prove* them wrong. We have to open this Hanukkah booth. Just think of it as practice for your own restaurant one day."

"I don't know—"

I looked at the smell cloud. The image of Siegel House Restaurant was so faded that I could barely make it out.

"Come on, Gigi," I said. "Trust me."

I stuck my hand out. "I promise I'll be there with you the whole time."

Gigi put her hand in mine. "Right next to me?"

I squeezed her hand. "I won't leave your side."

Finally, after hours of work, Gigi and I were done. We carefully packed up our donuts in boxes and put them on Gigi's red wagon. Gigi emptied her piggy bank into her pocket.

"It's my life's savings," she said. "Ten dollars and eighty-one cents."

Outside, the snow had frozen into thick patches of ice. We walked a few blocks to the entrance of the Hanukkah festival, trying not to slip.

There was a long line of businesses waiting to open a booth. People were selling all sorts of things: ceramic bowls, jewelry, candles, handmade soaps, latkes, you name it.

Finally, we got to the front of the line. I couldn't wait for everyone to taste our delicious menu. They were going to be so impressed!

But when it was our turn to claim a booth number, the man at the desk just looked straight past us.

"Next in line," he called.

The people behind us tried to cut ahead.

"Wait a second," said Gigi. "I'm next. I've been waiting in line."

The man frowned. "You're in line? For what exactly?"

"For a booth at the Hanukkah festival!" Gigi said. "Wait until you taste my donut recipes. They're absolutely scrumptious."

The man coughed a few times.

"Oh, no, this is a serious festival for serious businesses. Now run along," he said. "Next in line."

"But—" Gigi started.

She held out the money she'd been saving for ages. "I have money—just like everybody else. I'd like one booth, please."

The man looked stunned. His frown grew even deeper.

"I believe you should go home now. We don't rent booths to little girls. Where are your parents?"

What?

I felt like someone had hit me right in the gut.

I watched as the man motioned for the next business to come to the front of the line. Two boys, only slightly older than us, walked up to the desk. This just wasn't fair!

Next to me, Gigi's face grew pale.

I looked at her.

"This can't be happening," I said. "I mean, if they could just try our donuts, they would see.

Hey, why don't you give him a donut sample? It would—"

But Gigi cut me off. "No, that's enough, Saralee." She walked away from the line.

"Wait, Gigi," I called after her. "We have to do something. There has to be a way."

But Gigi wasn't listening. I ran to catch up with her.

"Gigi, stop—"

She turned around to face me.

"You were wrong," she said, her nostrils flaring. "This was one big mistake. Everyone's been trying to warn me all day . . . my father, the doctor, my mother . . . but I didn't listen."

"But what about your big dream?" I asked. "You know, you're going to open a restaurant one day."

Gigi crossed her arms. "I'm done dreaming."

It was silent for a moment. The sun was sinking into the horizon.

"Wait—" I started.

Gigi turned toward me. "No, Saralee. I've decided. It's time for you to go home."

Chapter Fifteen
A Normal Girl

I didn't know what to do or say. Back at Gigi's house, the smell cloud still hovered in the kitchen. I tried to see through to the other side, but the image was completely blurred now.

Gigi walked me over to the portal.

"Look," she said, taking my hand, "no matter what, I'm glad I met you. I never thought I'd meet someone with a nose like mine."

I swallowed. I didn't want to cry, but my eyes were filling up with tears. I didn't want to go home just yet. I didn't get enough time with her. And I had to make sure Gigi didn't give up on her big dream of opening her restaurant one day.

"Are you sure you want to give up?" I asked. My voice came out all squeaky.

Gigi nodded. "It's time for me to be what everyone else wants me to be . . . a normal girl. A normal girl with a regular nose and no crazy dreams."

Gigi let go of my hand, and I stepped into the smell cloud. I watched as the image of Gigi in her kitchen faded away. Again, I was surrounded by the whirling chocolate chips, bananas, and hazelnuts. The ingredients seemed duller now, less flavorful. That bitter smell overpowered them all.

I couldn't believe my time with Gigi had come to an end.

I stumbled out of the smell cloud to the other side. My whole body felt heavy, like a giant bag

of beans. I rubbed my eyes. I needed one of
Zadie's late-night cups of hot choco—

WAIT A MINUTE!

I whirled around, taking notice of my
surroundings. Where was I? This was *not* the
Siegel House kitchen.

My mind was reeling.

I was definitely back in the future—this
kitchen had a full refrigerator, double oven, and
a microwave. But it wasn't our kitchen. Not at

all! The walls were pink, and the counters were completely spotless. We never have spotless counters at Siegel House—*never!*

All of a sudden, Aunt Bean walked into the room carrying a bottle of cleaning spray and a rag.

"Oh Saralee," she said, smiling. "Be a dear and tidy up your toys in the playroom. I'm trying to deep clean."

Playroom?

We didn't have a playroom at Siegel House. There wasn't any space for a playroom with our big dining room on the ground floor and all of our bedrooms upstairs.

I tried to clear my head. None of this made any sense.

"Wait, Aunt Bean, where are we? Where's Zadie?" I blubbered.

Aunt Bean's eyebrows knit together. "Where are you? At home, silly. And we'll be visiting Zadie and Bubbie tomorrow for the Hanukkah party."

She started scrubbing the already clean

countertops. "The playroom, Saralee—"

In a daze, I left the kitchen and started down the hall. I felt this tingling in my chest like someone was scrambling eggs in there. Where was Siegel House Restaurant?

Around me, the hallway was decorated with photographs. I stopped and stared at the biggest one, a family portrait. We were all there— Bubbie, Zadie, Uncle Sam, Aunt Bean, Aunt Lotte, Josh, and me. But instead of standing in front of Siegel House Restaurant, we were in front of a different house. A very brown and boring house.

My hands grew clammy.

Oh no, oh no, OH NO!

I squeezed my eyes shut. This couldn't be happening! If Gigi never got the courage to open Siegel House Restaurant, then . . . there *wasn't* a Siegel House Restaurant anymore.

"This is a dream," I whispered to myself. "This has to be a dream."

"What's a dream?" said a voice.

I looked up to find my little cousin Josh staring at me. He was wearing his white lab coat and carried a toy doctor's bag in his hands.

"Ummm, nothing," I said.

Josh gave me a look. "Are you okay? Should I do an eezamination?"

He beckoned me forward, and I followed him into what must have been the playroom. I couldn't help but stare. The room was filled with decorated cardboard boxes.

Josh had turned the largest box into a makeshift doctor's office. He had painted the walls green, and he'd even cut a door and windows into the cardboard. Right next to it was a cardboard box ambulance.

He opened the ambulance door. "Have no fear, Dr. Josh is here!"

Shakily, I laid down inside the box. He took out a plastic magnifying glass from his doctor's kit and peered into my eyeballs.

"What hurts, Saralee?" Josh asked. "I'm here to help."

Chapter Sixteen
Doctor Supervision

What hurts?

I didn't even know where to begin. Siegel House was gone! This was an emergency! I needed to talk to Zadie immediately.

"Can you show me Zadie's room? I need to talk to him," I said.

Josh gave me a look and then took out his prescription pad. He started scribbling.

"Zadie's room? What room?"

"You know, the room Bubbie and Zadie sleep in."

Josh frowned. "What? They don't live here."

I swallowed. "They don't? But . . . why?"

"I don't know," shrugged Josh. "They've always lived at the Shalom Home. It's where all the old people live."

For a second, I felt like I couldn't breathe. Bubbie and Zadie didn't live with us anymore? "Well, what about Aunt Lotte?" I asked. "Does she live here?"

"Yeah—in the basement. Did you bump your head, Saralee?"

I took a deep sniff and tried to calm down. But even that didn't work. This house smelled different. Not like Siegel House at all. All of the familiar scents were gone—Zadie's evening cup of coffee, the sweet and sour pickles, Aunt Bean's display of rainbow-colored cookies. Instead, the house smelled . . . clean. Very, very clean.

I didn't say anything, so Josh started putting his doctor's tools away.

"You need a good night's sleep," he said.

"Doctor's orders. Don't worry; I'll take you home."

He rushed into the driver's seat of his ambulance and clutched the steering wheel. "Wheeeeeeeeee!" he shouted. "Stay clear! Ambulance coming through!"

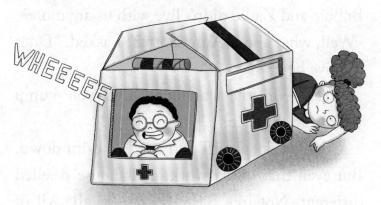

I closed my eyes. Maybe Josh was right? Maybe if I went to sleep, everything would go back to normal in the morning?

Josh pretended to park the ambulance and then pulled me to my feet. "This way, miss."

He rushed me upstairs into a very large bedroom. It was painted light purple and had a flowery bedspread with fluffy pillows.

Purple?

Flowers?

This was nothing like our real bedroom at Siegel House.

"This is our room?" I asked.

Josh laughed. "No, it's *your* room. My room is next door. Maybe you need medicine for your head?"

"Oh." I was so used to sharing a room with Josh, it would be weird to sleep without him. "Ummm, okay."

Josh turned to leave.

"Wait—" I called.

Josh turned around.

"I might need overnight doctor supervision. What if you sleep over? You know . . . to make sure I'm okay."

Josh grinned. "I'll go get my jammies. Be right back."

Chapter Seventeen

Stinky Eggs

The next morning, I woke up to something stinky. I wrinkled my nostrils, my eyes still heavy with sleep. Was that . . . burnt eggs?

I couldn't understand it! I mean, Zadie never *ever* burns his eggs. Most mornings, Zadie makes us all the "breakfast of champions" before the restaurant opens. There are fluffy scrambled eggs, crunchy toast dotted with butter, and a big helping of zesty, perfectly ripe berries.

I rubbed my eyes.

Then I saw purple—*purple walls.* I sat up, memories flooding back to me. I looked down at my flowery bedspread.

Oh no.

Oh no, no, NO!

I was still here—in this crazy reality without Siegel House Restaurant. I scrambled out of bed, narrowly avoiding a crash with Josh, who was still snuggled in a sleeping bag right next to my bed.

In a daze, I dashed down the stairs and into the kitchen. The smell of burnt eggs grew overwhelming. My uncle Sam was standing over a frying pan, trying to scrape a ruined omelet onto his plate.

For a moment, I just stood there and stared.

Uncle Sam looked . . . strange.

Instead of wearing his normal jeans and T-shirt, he was wearing a suit. He wore a red tie around his neck and even had on fancy shoes. I'd never seen him so dressed up!

"Oh snickerdoodle," Uncle Sam sighed, frowning at his ruined egg.

"Where are you going with that suit?" I blurted.

Uncle Sam twirled around, and the spatula flew out of his hands. It landed on the floor with a crash, getting bits of burnt egg on the floor.

"Golly gee willikers, you scared me," he said. "Going to the office, of course."

"The office?"

He nodded. "Yeah—you know, where I do my work."

In a rush, Uncle Sam grabbed his briefcase.

"Gotta skedaddle," he said quickly. "I've got a big meeting this morning. Can't be late."

And before I could ask any questions, he rushed down the hall and out the front door.

Just then, Aunt Bean walked into the kitchen. She immediately spied the bits of egg on the floor and dove for her cleaning solution. Today her T-shirt said "Bean Makes It Clean Company."

This was unbelievable! Instead of working all together at Siegel House, Aunt Bean had a cleaning company, and Uncle Sam worked in a fancy office? It was a completely different world!

A moment later, Aunt Lotte moped into the room. Well, at least *she* still looked the same, with her spiky hair and bedazzled T-shirt. She frowned as she poured herself a cup of coffee.

"Can't wait for the weekend," she grumbled to me. "Work is crazy these days. Way too many customers and way too many dishes."

Then she looked down at her watch. "Ugh, my shift started five minutes ago. Pass me my work apron, would you, Saralee?"

I turned around and saw a black apron hanging on a hook. I reached out to grab it and then froze in my tracks.

The apron had three letters on it.

P.O.P.

"Perfection on a Platter?" I cried. "Harold's restaurant? You work there?"

Aunt Bean took a big sip of coffee and rolled her eyes at me. "Very funny. Of course, I do. It's the only restaurant in town."

Haunted House

The rest of the morning was one disappointment after another. Zadie wasn't there to make us breakfast, so Josh and I ate healthy cereal that tasted like old socks. There were no early bird customers coming for the breakfast special. Bubbie wasn't around to greet the guests with a cheery smile. It was just so— BORING.

After breakfast, Josh and I walked to school together. We got a little lost because this house was in a different part of the neighborhood than Siegel House. But eventually, I found Main Street and knew exactly where I was.

"Hey, we're not late, right?" I asked Josh.

He shook his head.

I grabbed his hand. "I want to take a little detour."

Josh followed behind me, clutching his doctor's bag in his other hand. Maybe Siegel House Restaurant was still there? I just had to see with my own eyes. We turned right, then left, and then right again.

Siegel House should be right around the corner . . .

I stopped.

It felt like a big clump of oatmeal sunk to the pit of my stomach.

Siegel House was . . . it was an old, abandoned building. The front door was hanging off the hinges. The paint was cracked and peeling. And thick spider webs hung from the windows.

The world seemed to spin around me. *This*
was my beautiful restaurant?

"Why are we at the haunted house?" asked
Josh.

I turned toward him. "Wait—what?"

He nodded, his eyes all wide. "Yeah—no
one comes here. There's a ghost in there."

I just stood there, trying to breathe in and

out. The air here smelled stale and musty—like the whole house was covered in damp, rotting wood.

My heart sank in my chest. A creepy haunted house . . . that's what our restaurant had become.

For the rest of the walk, I couldn't get the image of the abandoned building out of my mind. I guess Gigi had never bought the house and turned it into a restaurant. So the building was just rotting away.

When I got to my classroom, I headed straight to my seat. I turned to look for Harold, but he was sitting at a different desk across the room.

I rushed over to him. "Hey, Harold, I have to tell you something!"

He looked up. "Huh?'

"I need to tell you something crazy," I said again. "You will never believe what my super-nose did."

Harold gave me a funny look. "What're you talking about?"

I sighed. "My nose! My super-nose did something crazy."

Harold looked really puzzled. "Your super-nose? What do you mean? You like . . . never talk to me."

"I—what?"

Harold went back to his cookbook. "What's your name again, Sararose?"

"It's—it's Saralee," I said aghast. "Harold, this isn't funny. Of course I've told you about my super-nose. You're my best friend."

Just then, Jacob Brodsky sat down next to Harold.

"How's it going, man?" he asked, bumping fists with Harold. "You still gonna make that

cake with the Hanukkah story on it? Can't wait to eat a slice."

Harold turned away from me and started chatting with Jacob.

WHAT?

It couldn't be!

Harold was best friends with Jacob? I felt this sinking feeling in the pit of my stomach. But . . . I guess it made sense. In the *real* world, Harold and I had bonded over both having restaurants. And here . . . I didn't have a restaurant. I guess we'd never gotten to know each other.

The rest of the day went by in a blur. By the time Josh and I arrived home, I felt totally numb— like when you drink something really cold and your whole mouth gets tingly.

I sat in the playroom with Josh until it was time to go to the Hanukkah party. Terrible thoughts raced through my mind. What if in this reality Zadie was . . . different? What if he wasn't the world's number one grandpa here? What if he didn't love me the same way?

Chapter Nineteen
Shalom Home

The Shalom Home was nice, I guess. The lobby had squashy armchairs, a piano, and a huge fish tank. Hanukkah decorations covered the walls, and there was a menorah in every window. Each one had six unlit candles.

I took a little sniff. Yuck! The whole place smelled like bleach and cherry Jell-O.

Bubbie and Zadie were waiting for us on the couch.

"Oh my Pookie Wookies," Bubbie exclaimed. "It's been so long."

I held my breath, waiting for Zadie to speak.

But instead, he got down on one knee and pulled Josh and me into a tight squeeze. I took a deep breath. He smelled just the same, like peppermint with the slightest bit of corned beef on rye.

"I've missed you," he said.

I let out my breath and looked into his eyes—they were big and brown, and warm like butter. Thank the stars, he was just the same.

Soon the party began. Each family lit their own menorah and got to play dreidel. Dreidel is usually a pretty fun game, but I was grumpy the entire time. Josh couldn't wait his turn and kept eating all the chocolate gelt.

After the game, everyone got in line for some donuts and latkes.

Well, everyone except for me.

I didn't have an appetite.

"What's wrong, Saralee?" asked Zadie,

coming toward me. "You seem down."

He sat next to me. For a moment, we were alone, just the two of us.

"You can tell me—" said Zadie quietly.

I wanted to talk to him, I really did. But how could I tell him that Siegel House Restaurant disappeared? In this reality, Zadie would have no idea what I was talking about.

"I just—" I started. "I just don't know what to do."

Zadie leaned in closer. "About what?"

"It's one of my friends," I explained. "I'm . . . I'm really worried about her. She doesn't believe in herself at all. She used to have big dreams about opening a restaurant one day. But she decided to give it all up. It's really bothering me. I don't think she should quit!"

Zadie scratched his chin. "A restaurant, you say?"

"Yeah," I nodded. "It's a really cool restaurant idea too. There'd be an unlimited pickle bar, a glass display with all sorts of rainbow cookies, and a bunch of huge sandwiches on the menu."

Zadie's eyes grew wide. "Golly, sounds like my kind of restaurant. An unlimited pickle bar? I'd eat there every day."

"Me too," I said. "But she's completely given up on it. A lot of people told her she couldn't do it, and she never stands up for herself."

It was quiet for a moment, and then Zadie pointed at the glowing menorah.

"Remember in the Hanukkah story when the Maccabees used their strength as fighters to stand up for themselves?"

I nodded.

"Well, *everyone* has something they're good at. What do you think your friend's strength is? Maybe there's a way you can encourage her to use it?"

I let that sink in for a moment.

What was Gigi's strength?

Well, it was the same as mine—her super-nose abilities, of course. That girl could smell things like no one's business.

I looked up at Zadie.

"But what if she doesn't want to use her strength anymore?" I asked.

Zadie wrapped his arm around my shoulder. "That's where you come in. You've got to show her how much she matters; how much the world needs people like her."

I gave Zadie a big squeeze.

"I think maybe I can find a way to do that," I said quietly.

"You can do anything," said Zadie. "That, I know for sure."

Chapter Twenty
By Heart

When we got home from the party, I headed straight to the kitchen.

Aunt Bean and Uncle Sam had just turned on a movie in the living room. Aunt Lotte was gabbing on the phone in the basement. And Josh was giving his stuffed animals some check-ups in the playroom.

This was my chance! No one would notice if I did a little baking.

I scurried through the cabinets, looking for

the right ingredients. Good thing Aunt Bean is really organized! Each drawer was labeled with perfect handwriting.

By now, I knew Gigi's Hanukkah Donuts recipe by heart. It took me only a few minutes to whip up the dough. Like clockwork, my super-nose began to buzz and tingle. I watched as the smell cloud appeared in the air.

The smell of Gigi's donuts washed over me. It was time to bring my restaurant back.

"Saralee? What're you doing here?" Gigi's voice sounded strange.

She stood at the kitchen counter, staring at me. She was holding a plate with just a few donuts on it. And on her nose was a clothespin. It was pinching her nostrils together!

"What are you doing?" I gasped. "Why would you ever do that to your nose?"

"You heard the doctor," she said in a nasally voice. "This is one of my exercises. Why are you back, Saralee? I thought you went home."

I rushed over to her. "I needed to come back."

I looked around the room. The golden menorah still stood in the windowsill. Six glowing candles filled the room with a flickering light. I guess a full day had gone by here, as well.

I pointed to the plate of donuts. "Have you changed your mind? Are you going to make more donuts to sell?"

Gigi shook her head. "No. I'm just feeling down. It's this clothespin—it's driving me bonkers. And baking is the only thing that makes me feel better."

Suddenly, I felt angry—like my whole body was a scalding hot oven.

I reached out and yanked the clothespin off of Gigi's nose.

"Hey!" she yelled.

I clenched the clothespin in my fist and glared at her.

"Look, this isn't a game," I said. "When I went back through the portal, my whole life was different. The restaurant was gone. My family was weird. I didn't even have a best friend anymore."

Gigi shook her head. "I don't understand, what does that have to do with me?"

I couldn't believe this!

It had EVERYTHING to do with her!

"Are you kidding?" I said angrily. "My restaurant was created by *YOU*. And you quit your dream. Now my restaurant is gone, and my life is just . . ."

I swallowed.

How could I explain what I'd lost?

I took a deep sniff, trying to calm down.

"Look, everyone has a strength, something they're good at," I explained. "And yours is your super-nose."

I held up the clothespin. "Do you really want

to spend the rest of your life making everyone else happy? Doing things you hate? Having a super-nose is part of who you are! You'll be miserable if you get rid of it. You have to be brave!"

Gigi stood very still.

I walked over and clasped her hand in mine. I thought back to what Zadie had said when he told me about my super-nose. "You gotta develop your smell powers in your own way. Be your own person. You know?"

At first, she didn't say anything. But then she looked up at me.

"When I use my super-nose," she said quietly, "it's like the whole world lights up. It's like my only way to show people who I am and what I feel on the inside. I've been wearing this clothespin for a day now. And everything just seems . . . darker."

I nodded. "That's why you can't give up, Gigi. You just can't."

She looked up at me. "But I have no choice.

We've tried everything, and it just didn't work."

I smiled.

"Not quite everything," I said. "Get the ingredients back out of the cupboard. I have an idea!"

An hour later, we packed up our freshly made donuts in Gigi's red wagon. It had begun to flurry outside. Soft snowflakes drifted to the ground.

"I still don't understand what we're doing," said Gigi, as we pulled the wagon. "We can't open up a booth at the festival. That man said so."

"We're not opening a booth," I said with a mysterious smile.

"Then what are we doing?" asked Gigi.

"You'll see."

We pulled the wagon right outside of the festival's gates. I could hear music and the sound of children laughing. But we didn't go inside the festival. Instead, we parked our wagon on the sidewalk.

People walked by, giving us strange looks.

"Ummm, what's going on, Saralee?" asked Gigi. "We're not selling the donuts *here*, are we? I mean, this isn't professional at all. No one's going to buy them."

"Just you wait," I said.

I leaned down and opened one of the boxes of donuts. The smell of Gigi's donuts swirled into the air.

Chapter Twenty-One
Follow the Scent

"**L**et's use our noses," I said. "Let's make the donuts smell so *powerful*, the customers come to us instead."

"But . . . I've never done that before," said Gigi.

"Oh yes you have," I said. That first night I met you—I smelled your Hanukkah donuts from years and YEARS in the future!"

Gigi looked confused. "What do you mean? How do you know you weren't just smelling your own cooking?"

I felt snowflakes landing gently on my eyelashes.

"Because," I said. "When I made your Hanukkah donut recipe, I didn't just smell the ingredients. I smelled something else; something sad, something just a little bit bitter. Your super-nose added those feelings—of all those times your dad, and your mom, and the doctor, and those girls from school put down your dreams. And I *felt* a little bit of what you were feeling, even from years away."

Gigi's eyes grew wide. "Oh . . ."

"Trust me, your nose is powerful," I said. "We can do this!"

Gigi took a deep breath. "Okay. Then let's do it."

She closed her eyes, and I did the same. Then with all my might, I imagined the smell particles of our donuts floating up and outward. My super-nose tingled, and the smell of donuts took over my nostrils.

With my eyes squeezed shut, I could just

imagine the scent of our donuts wafting through the entrance of the Hanukkah festival, over all the booths and businesses.

"Wow," Gigi breathed.

I peeked an eye open.

Around us, people stopped in their tracks, looking up.

"What's that delicious smell?" called someone in the distance.

"Who's selling donuts?"

A few feet away, a woman looked in our direction.

She sniffed.

Then she sniffed again.

Slowly, she walked toward us. "Is that smell coming from your wagon?"

Gigi turned and stared.

I motioned for her to say something.

"You have your first customer," I whispered.

"It's ummm . . . well it's my . . . ummm I'm selling Hanukkah donuts. Would you like one?" Gigi asked.

The woman wrinkled her eyebrows. "*You're* selling them? Did you make these? They smell absolutely heavenly. The scent is so strong!"

Gigi nodded. "Four cents if you want one."

The woman opened her purse.

By this time, a small crowd had gathered around us.

"I'll take one," a man exclaimed.

"I'll take one too!"

I watched Gigi's face as she handed out the

donuts. At first, she looked nervous. Her hands were shaking, and she kept biting her lips. But then, as more people approached her, she looked more and more relaxed.

"I just can't believe this," said a woman as she took another bite. "It tastes . . . just so hopeful. I feel excited, alive!"

All of a sudden, a man approached the wagon.

Gigi looked up. Her eyes grew wide.

Uh-oh.

"Father?" Gigi squeaked.

This was not good! Gigi's father was carrying a stack of presents wrapped in shiny paper. He must have bought them at the Hanukkah festival.

Terrible thoughts raced through my mind.

What if he told Gigi to go home? Would Siegel House Restaurant be lost forever?

Gigi's father looked around at all of the people eating donuts. He opened his mouth to speak but then closed it again.

"My goodness, this is the best donut I've ever tasted," one of the customers said to Gigi's father. "What a daughter you have!"

"Will you sell more tomorrow?" a woman asked Gigi.

"I can bring you a table to use," said another customer.

"Oh, and I have a sign," said someone else. "You can write 'Donuts for Sale.'"

Gigi looked at me. Then she looked at her dad.

I could tell she was thinking about what to say.

"Be brave, Gigi," I whispered to her.

She nodded at me. And slowly, she lifted her head high and said in a loud voice, "Yes, I'll be back tomorrow—this time with way more donuts."

I grinned.

Gigi's father pressed his lips together.

He looked around at all the happy customers and then back at his daughter. He ran his hand through his hair.

Then, he reached out.

"Can I try one?" he asked softly.

Gigi beamed. "Absolutely. And for you, it's free."

Chapter Twenty-Two
Our Restaurant

Before we knew it, the donuts were completely gone. We started pulling the empty wagon back to Gigi's house.

"Did you see how many people wanted to buy MY donuts?" Gigi gushed.

"Wait until tomorrow," I said. "There'll be way more people. News about an exciting new recipe always travels fast."

Gigi took the clothespin out of her pocket and threw it in a nearby trash can.

"I'm done with that," she said, grinning.

We spent the rest of the walk talking about Gigi's donut menu for tomorrow. But even though I was excited for Gigi, I had this nervous feeling in the pit of my stomach.

Had we done enough?

Was Siegel House Restaurant back?

When we got back to Gigi's house, my whole body felt like a twisty pretzel. Gigi was still chattering away, but I was barely listening.

She went into the kitchen.

I hesitated to follow.

What if the smell portal hadn't changed? What if Siegel House was truly gone forever?

Gigi poked her head out of the kitchen. "Come on, Saralee—let's plan the menu for tomorrow."

"I ummm—"

Gigi grabbed my hand and pulled me into the kitchen. The smell cloud was still there, hovering like a giant sphere of light.

My legs felt wobbly as I looked through to the other side.

I could see . . .

Siegel House Restaurant was back! My heart began to melt like chocolate chips in a warm pan. I could see the outline of our kitchen, crystal clear.

In that moment, I missed home so badly, I could barely breathe. I wanted to cook with Zadie again and eat leftovers with Uncle Sam. I wanted to see the customers, and fold napkins, and help Aunt Bean frost the cookies.

"So what donut flavors should we make tomorrow?" asked Gigi.

I took a step toward the smell cloud.

"I'm sorry, Gigi," I said. "But I think it's time for me to go home."

"Already?" Gigi asked.

I nodded and looked at the smell cloud. An idea crossed my mind.

"Hey, do you want to see it?" I asked her.

Gigi blinked. "See what?"

"Your restaurant," I said. "The one you're going to make one day."

At first, Gigi just stared. "I can . . . I can see it?"

I pointed at the smell cloud. The image of the Siegel House kitchen was crisp and clear.

"Of course," I said. "Come through the portal, just for a minute."

Gigi tucked one of her curls behind her ears. "Okay," she said. "I guess it wouldn't hurt."

I took her hand, but she stayed rooted to the spot. "Don't worry. You're going to love it, okay? Trust me," I said.

Gigi took a shaky step forward. And together, we stepped into the smell cloud. The scent of Gigi's donuts wrapped around us like a blanket. I closed my eyes, relishing the scent, trying to take it all in. The smell of bitterness had completely disappeared. Now the recipe smelled light and refreshing . . . full of hope and courage.

When we stepped through the other side, I looked around at Siegel House Restaurant! Everything was in its place—the platters of latkes on the counters, Zadie's coffee mugs in the sink, and the drawers stuffed with our family recipes.

I looked over at Gigi.

She was standing very still, her eyes wide.

"Here, come take a look," I said, pulling her toward the door that led to the dining room. I opened it just a crack so we could see out.

Siegel House was a sight to behold.

Tonight, the dining room was packed with customers. Every single seat was taken. Gigi stared at the pickle bar and at the glass dessert display filled with cookies. She stared at the finely set tables and the sign that said "Siegel House Restaurant."

"I—I made all this?" she breathed.

"Every bit," I said.

Gigi's eyes lingered on the menorah in the window.

"Is that my family's menorah?" she asked, pointing.

I laughed out loud. "You mean *our* family's menorah? Yes, I guess it is."

For a few minutes, we just stood there, side by side, watching the hustle and bustle of our restaurant.

"I wish you could stay forever," I finally said. "Imagine all the cooking we could do."

Gigi nodded. "I wish I could stay too. But—"

She looked around the kitchen again. "If I'm going to make all this, I have a lot of work to do too."

We started walking back toward the smell cloud. Gigi pulled me into a tight hug.

"Goodbye, Saralee," she said.

I squeezed her tighter. "Bye, Gigi."

I watched as she disappeared through the portal. The smell cloud began to fade away.

It was quiet for a moment. And in the silence, I relished the smells of the Siegel House kitchen. Latkes with applesauce and sour cream, donuts with rainbow sprinkles, noodles, and kugels, and hot chocolate with whipped cream. Finally, I was home.

Suddenly, the kitchen door swung open.

"Ohhhhhhhh Saralee," called Zadie. "How are those peanut butter and jelly donuts coming along?"

I smiled.

I could hear songs and laughter coming from the dining room.

"They'll be done soon," I called back.

I took a deep breath with my super-nose. It was time to get back to work.

The End

Gigi's Hanukkah Donuts

Makes 20–24 donuts

Before making these donuts, ask an adult for permission. Always have an adult help when you need to use a knife or the stove. Be careful—hot oil is dangerous.

Ingredients

1 tablespoon instant/rapid-rise
  or active dry yeast
3 cups all-purpose flour, plus
  more for dusting
1 cup powdered sugar
¾ teaspoon salt
½ teaspoon ground nutmeg

2 large egg yolks
1 teaspoon vanilla extract
2 quarts vegetable oil
1 medium banana
¾ cup Nutella
1 tablespoon creamy
  peanut butter

(Gigi melted chocolate chips and added ground hazelnuts, but you can use Nutella.
—Saralee)

Making the dough

1. Combine 1 cup warm water and yeast in a small bowl, and let sit for 5 minutes until foamy.

2. Meanwhile, combine the flour, ¼ cup powdered sugar, salt, and nutmeg in a large bowl.

3. Separate the egg whites and yolks. Whisk the egg yolks, vanilla, and 2 tablespoons oil into the yeast/water mixture. (Save the egg whites for another recipe.)

4. Add the liquid mixture to the flour mixture, and stir until the dough comes together. It should be a bit sticky. Cover the bowl with plastic wrap, and let rise at room temperature for 1–2 hours, until doubled in size.

Frying the donuts

5. Dust a clean countertop and your hands with flour. Scrape the dough onto the counter, and dust it with flour too. Roll the dough into a ¼-inch thick rectangle. Use a cookie cutter or drinking glass to cut the dough into 2½-inch circles. Sprinkle the circles lightly with flour.

6. Add enough oil to a large Dutch oven or heavy pot to measure about 2 inches deep. Ask an adult to heat the oil over medium heat to 350°F. (If you don't have a deep-fry thermometer, test the temperature by dropping in a 1-inch cube of bread; the oil is ready if the bread turns golden brown in about 1 minute.)

7. Ask an adult to fry the dough: Using a slotted spoon, carefully place 6 dough pieces in the oil, and fry until golden brown, about 3 minutes, flipping halfway through. Using a slotted spoon, transfer the donuts to a baking sheet lined with paper towels. Repeat with the remaining dough.

Finishing the donuts

8. For the filling, mash the banana in a medium bowl with a fork. Stir in ¾ cup Nutella. Ask an adult to use a paring knife to cut a small slit in the side of each donut to form a pocket in the center. Scoop 1–2 teaspoons of filling inside.

9. For the drizzle, combine 3–4 teaspoons of water, ¾ cup powdered sugar, and the peanut butter in a small bowl. With a spoon, drizzle it onto the finished donuts. Serve warm.

127

Elana Rubinstein is the author of the Saralee Siegel books, *Once Upon an Apple Cake*, a National Jewish Book Award finalist, and *Starlight Soup*. She is an early childhood educator in Los Angeles, California.

Jennifer Naalchigar also illustrated *Once Upon an Apple Cake* and *Starlight Soup*. She has been drawing ever since she was old enough to hold a pencil. She lives in Hertfordshire, England.